Dear Parent:

Your child's love of reading sta~~

Every child learns to read in a different way and at ... or her own speed. Some go back and forth between reading levels and read favorite books again and again. Others read through each level in order. You can help your young reader improve and become more confident by encouraging his or her own interests and abilities. From books your child reads with you to the first books he or she reads alone, there are I Can Read Books for every stage of reading:

SHARED READING
Basic language, word repetition, and whimsical illustrations, ideal for sharing with your emergent reader

BEGINNING READING
Short sentences, familiar words, and simple concepts for children eager to read on their own

READING WITH HELP
Engaging stories, longer sentences, and language play for developing readers

READING ALONE
Complex plots, challenging vocabulary, and high-interest topics for the independent reader

I Can Read Books have introduced children to the joy of reading since 1957. Featuring award-winning authors and illustrators and a fabulous cast of beloved characters, I Can Read Books set the standard for beginning readers.

A lifetime of discovery begins with the magical words "I Can Read!"

Visit www.icanread.com for information on enriching your child's reading experience.

My Little Pony: Meet the Ponies of Maretime Bay
MY LITTLE PONY and HASBRO and all related trademarks and logos are trademarks of Hasbro, Inc.
©2022 Hasbro.
All rights reserved. Printed in the United States of America.
No part of this book may be used or reproduced in any manner whatsoever without written permission
except in the case of brief quotations embodied in critical articles and reviews.
For information addressHarperCollins Children's Books, a division of HarperCollins Publishers,
195 Broadway, New York, NY 10007.
www.icanread.com

Library of Congress Control Number: 2022937884
ISBN 978-0-06-303753-3

Book design by Elaine Lopez-Levine

22 23 24 25 26   LSCC   10 9 8 7 6 5 4 3 2 1   ❖   First Edition

MY LITTLE PONY

Meet the PONIES of MARETIME BAY

By Steve Foxe

HARPER

An Imprint of HarperCollinsPublishers

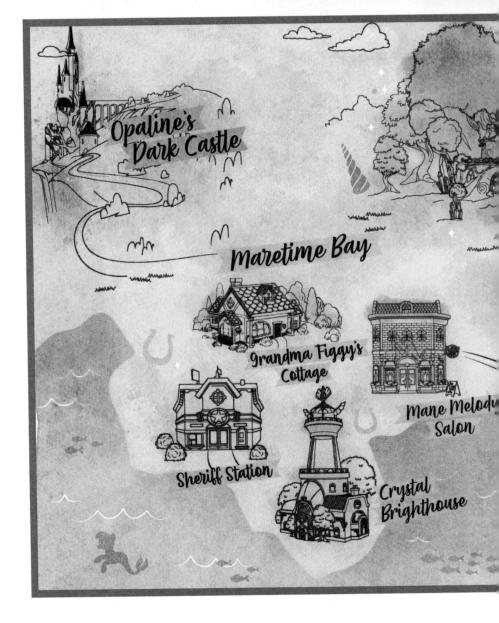

Opaline's Dark Castle

Maretime Bay

Grandma Figgy's Cottage

Mane Melody Salon

Sheriff Station

Crystal Brighthouse

For many moons,

Equestria had lost its magic.

The Earth Ponies,

Pegasi, and Unicorns

stayed far away from each other.

The Earth Ponies of Maretime Bay
used to fear magic.
But Sunny Starscout believed
in peace with the Pegasi
and unity with the Unicorns.
Now everypony is welcome!

Sunny and her friends
love to go on adventures
and spend time together.
They hang out at
the Crystal Brighthouse
on the tip of Maretime Bay.

Sunny's Hope Lantern helped reunite the Earth Ponies, Pegasi, and Unicorns.

Now she glides through Maretime Bay on her roller skates selling smoothies!

Sunny is an Earth Pony
with her own special magic.
When she helps others,
she turns into an Alicorn!
That means she has glowing
wings and a horn.

Hitch Trailblazer is the sheriff of Maretime Bay. He takes his job very seriously, especially when Earth Ponies are testing out their new magic!

Hitch has the magical ability
to understand critters.

Critters follow him
everywhere he goes!
He takes care of a baby dragon
called Sparky.

Izzy Moonbow always stood out
from the other Unicorns.

So she left the land of Unicorns
to meet different ponies
in Maretime Bay.

Izzy loves to craft.

She is always making creative gifts

for her pony friends.

So sweet!

Pipp Petals is a princess
and a pop star,
so she loves to be
the center of attention.

Her bedroom in
the Crystal Brighthouse
even looks like a stage!

Pipp loves music, fashion,

and makeovers.

She has fans across Equestria.

Zipp Storm is Pipp's sister
and a Pegasus princess too.
Zipp isn't ready to settle down
into the royal life just yet.

Zipp's room in the
Crystal Brighthouse
is as cool as she is!

It's the best place to
test out new flying tricks.
Zipp is one brave pony!

Everypony in Maretime Bay is different.

That's what makes it so special!

Sunny, Izzy, Pipp, Zipp, and Hitch are unique but they have one thing in common. They are all best friends!